Detective Dan

by Vivian French
illustrated by Alison Bartlett

PICTURE WINDOW BOOKS
Minneapolis, Minnesota

Editor: Jill Kalz
Page Production: Melissa Kes
Creative Director: Keith Griffin
Editorial Director: Carol Jones
Series Consultant: Sue Ellis

First American edition published in 2006 by
Picture Window Books
5115 Excelsior Boulevard
Suite 232
Minneapolis, MN 55416
877-845-8392
www.picturewindowbooks.com

First published in Great Britain by
A & C Black Publishers Ltd
37 Soho Square, London, W1D 3QZ
www.acblack.com
Text copyright © 2004 Vivian French
Illustrations copyright © 2004 Alison Bartlett

Printed in the United States of America.

Library of Congress Cataloging-in-Publication Data
French, Vivian.
Detective Dan / by Vivian French ; illustrated by Alison Bartlett.
p. cm. — (Read-it! chapter books)
Summary: Billy plays detective to find out who keeps knocking his
best friend Dan's lunchbox off the shelf at school and getting Dan
into trouble, but it is Dan who finally solves the mystery.
ISBN 1-4048-1659-3 (hardcover)
[1. Best friends—Fiction. 2. Friendship—Fiction. 3. Schools—Fiction.
4. Cats—Fiction. 5. Mystery and detective stories.] I. Bartlett, Alison,
ill. II. Title. III. Series.
PZ7.F88917Det 2005
[E]—dc22   2005030015

Table of Contents

For Ross

Chapter One

Dan and Billy were best friends. They walked to school together every morning. Every afternoon they ran home together. They did everything together.

One Monday afternoon, Dan came out of school very slowly.

"What's the matter, Dan?" asked his mom, Mrs. Wilson.

"Someone threw his lunch box on the floor," Billy told her.

"Maybe it just fell off the shelf," Mrs. Wilson said.

"Mrs. Harper said Dan was messy," Billy said.

"But I'm not!" said Dan. "I'm not messy!"

Dan frowned and grumbled all the way home.

On Tuesday afternoon, Dan came out of school even more slowly than he had on Monday.

"What's the matter, Dan?" Mrs. Wilson asked.

"Someone threw his lunch box on the floor *again*," said Billy.

"I'm sure they didn't mean to," said Mrs. Wilson. "Did you eat your sandwiches, Dan?"

"No," said Dan. "I didn't feel hungry at all."

"Mrs. Harper says Dan is getting *very* messy," Billy told Mrs. Wilson.

"And she said that I shouldn't talk to Minnie!" Dan said.

"Is Minnie the school cat?" Mrs. Wilson asked.

"Yes," Dan answered. "It's not fair. I don't mean to talk to Minnie, but Minnie always comes to talk to me!"

Dan frowned and grumbled all the way home again.

On Wednesday afternoon, Dan and Billy rushed out of school.

"Someone nibbled on Dan's sardine sandwiches!" Billy told Mrs. Wilson.

"Yes," said Dan. "Someone threw my lunch box on the floor. Someone threw everything out of it. Someone nibbled on one of my sardine sandwiches, and now I'm really hungry!"

"What did Mrs. Harper say?" asked Mrs. Wilson.

"I didn't tell her," Dan said.

"Why not?" Mrs. Wilson asked.

"She was upset," Dan said. "Minnie came into the classroom with me."

"Mrs. Harper said Dan let Minnie in, but he didn't," Billy said. "The cat just followed him."

"We'd better get you something to eat," said Mrs. Wilson.

"How about some extra-big sardine sandwiches!" said Dan.

Chapter Two

On Thursday morning, Dan walked slowly to school.

"I think I should hide my lunch box today," he told Billy. "Then no one can eat my delicious sardine sandwiches."

"You don't have sardine sandwiches today, Dan," Mrs. Wilson said. "I made you cheese sandwiches instead."

Billy suddenly stopped.

"I know!" he said. "I'll be a detective! I'll look for clues. I'll find out who pushed your lunch box off the shelf and tell Mrs. Harper. Then she won't blame you."

"Good idea!" said Dan, and they ran all the way to school.

Dan and Billy ran into the playground.

"Look!" said Billy. "There's Minnie!"

Dan called, "Minnie! Here, kitty, kitty, kitty!"

Minnie came running. She ran in and out of Dan's legs and around and around his school bag. But when he tried to pick her up, she wriggled and struggled.

Mrs. Harper walked past them.

"Now, Dan," she said. "I don't want Minnie in school. Put her down, please."

Dan put Minnie down, and she
quickly ran away.

"Why doesn't Minnie like me today?" Dan asked.

"I'll find out!" Billy told him. "I'm a detective!"

"You've got to find out about my lunch box first," Dan said.

When it was time for class, Dan and Billy hurried inside.

They put their lunch boxes on
the shelf outside the classroom.
Then they sat down at their table
for reading time.

"Be sure to watch for clues!"
Billy whispered.

Dan nodded.

"No whispering!" Mrs. Harper
said sternly.

Billy put his hand up.

"May I please go to the bathroom?" he asked.

Mrs. Harper frowned. "Do you really have to go, Billy?"

"Yes, Mrs. Harper," Billy said, nodding his head.

"What were you doing?" Dan whispered when Billy came back to his desk.

"Looking for clues," Billy whispered. "You go next!"

Dan put his hand up.

"May I please go to the bathroom?" he asked.

Mrs. Harper frowned again.

"Do you really have to go?"

Dan nodded.

"Did you see anything?" Billy whispered when Dan came back.

"My lunch box is still there," Dan whispered back.

Mrs. Harper folded her arms. "Billy and Dan," she said. "I do not like whispering in my classroom! You two will stay inside at recess!"

Billy smiled. "Thank you, Mrs. Harper," he said.

Mrs. Harper looked at him and raised her eyebrows.

"What are you two up to?" she asked.

"Nothing, Mrs. Harper," Billy said, still smiling.

"Billy's a detective," Dan explained. "He's going to find out who's been throwing my lunch box on the floor."

"I see," Mrs. Harper said. "Well, no more whispering! And you can sit in here and read *quietly* at recess. Is that understood?"

Chapter Three

At recess time, Dan got his book and sat down. Billy sat down, too. But when Mrs. Harper left the room, Billy jumped up again.

"Let's look for fingerprints," he said.

"How?" Dan asked.

Billy thought for a moment. "We'll put chalk dust on all of the lunch boxes," he said. "Then we'll see everybody's fingerprints!"

"But won't the chalk dust be messy?" Dan asked.

"We need to find a clue," Billy told him.

"OK," said Dan.

Billy picked up the chalkboard eraser and sprinkled chalk dust over the lunch boxes.

"There!" Billy said. "Now we'll see everybody's fingerprints!"

At lunch time, Billy and Dan watched carefully as everybody else collected their boxes.

"Yuck!" said Molly. "My lunch box is all dusty!"

"ACHOO! ACHOO!" sneezed Ben. "So is mine!"

All of the children began blowing off the chalk dust.

"ACHOO! ACHOO! ACHOO!" they sneezed.

Mrs. Harper came to see what was going on.

"Dan!" she said sternly. "Does this have something to do with you and Billy?"

Dan looked at Billy. Billy looked at the floor.

"Mrs. Harper, we were looking for fingerprints," Dan explained.

Mrs. Harper frowned her most terrible frown. "I think," she said, "you two had better stop being detectives *right now*!"

At the end of the afternoon,
Dan and Billy walked out of school
very slowly.

Mrs. Wilson was waiting for
them at the school gate.

"What's the matter now?" she
asked. "Did somebody eat your
sandwiches again?"

"No," Dan said. "Nobody took my lunch box today."

"Mrs. Harper was very, very upset," Billy said.

Dan nodded.

"We had to stay inside at recess and lunch time," Billy said.

"Mrs. Harper didn't read us a story in the afternoon," Dan said.

"Everyone had dusty clothes," Billy said. "So they were pretty upset, too."

"It's not fair," said Dan, and he grumbled all the way home.

Billy walked home behind him.

Chapter Four

On Friday morning, Dan walked to school very slowly.

"Cheer up," Mrs. Wilson said. "I made you an extra-big sardine sandwich today."

Dan didn't cheer up.

"I'll be a detective again!" Billy said. "I'll find out about your lunch box!"

"No," Dan said. "I don't like that game. I don't like it at all!"

Dan didn't cheer up when Minnie came to meet him in the playground.

He didn't cheer up when he went inside.

He put his lunch box on the shelf and sat down at his table with a sigh.

"Cheer up, Dan," said Mrs. Harper. "Things will get better."

Dan didn't answer. He picked up his book and read quietly.

Billy looked at Dan, and then he picked up his book, too.

Dan was very quiet all morning. When it was time for lunch, he stayed sitting at his table. Billy stayed, too.

"Come along, you two," said Mrs. Harper. "Get your lunch boxes and zoom down to the cafeteria with everyone else!"

"I'll get your lunch box, Dan," Billy said. He went out of the door and couldn't believe his eyes.

There was only one lunch box left on the shelf.

"Mrs. Harper," Billy shouted, "come quick! Somebody took Dan's lunch box again!"

Mrs. Harper found Dan's empty
lunch box by the garbage.

Dan found his carton of juice
behind a chair.

Billy found Dan's apple and
carrot sticks under a table.

But sadly, there was no sign
of Dan's extra-big sardine
sandwich anywhere.

"Dear me," Mrs. Harper said.

"You can share my sandwiches,"
Billy said.

"No, thank you," said Dan.
"I'm not hungry."

Chapter Five

After lunch, Mrs. Harper asked all of the students to sit down. She asked if anyone had taken Dan's sandwich. All of the children shook their heads.

"What kind of sandwich was it, Dan?" Mrs. Harper asked.

"Sardine," said Dan.

Everyone made a face.

"No one likes sardines except Dan," Billy said.

"Is that true?" asked Mrs.
Harper, looking around the room.

Everyone nodded.

Mrs. Harper looked at Dan.
"Well, Dan! I don't know what to
say. Maybe we do need a detective
after all!"

Dan didn't answer. He was looking through the open classroom door.

"Are you listening to me, Dan?" Mrs. Harper asked.

Dan suddenly smiled a huge smile. "Mrs. Harper, I know who ate my sardine sandwich!" he said. "It was *Minnie*!"

Mrs. Harper shook her head and said, "Oh no, Dan. I'm sure she didn't!"

"Yes!" said Dan. "She liked me on Monday. On Tuesday, she followed me into school. On Wednesday, my sandwich was nibbled on. But she didn't like me yesterday, and that's because I had a cheese sandwich. Today, I brought sardines again, and she liked me."

Dan looked sad and said, "I thought Minnie liked *me*, but she really just liked my sardine sandwiches. Look!" Dan pointed out the door.

Mrs. Harper looked. So did Billy and all of the children in the class. They gasped.

Minnie was up on the lunch box shelf. She was walking in and out of the empty boxes, sniffing. Suddenly, she stopped.

"That's my lunch box!" Dan whispered.

Minnie pushed at the box with her paw.

CRASH!

It fell on the floor and opened.
Minnie jumped down and climbed
inside. She was purring loudly.

"Well, I don't believe it," said
Mrs. Harper. "Well done,
Detective Dan!"

The children cheered.

"Next week, Dan, you'd better keep your lunch box *inside* the classroom!" Mrs. Harper said.

Dan nodded.

Mrs. Harper smiled and said, "I'm sorry I said you were messy, Dan. And I'm sure Minnie is sorry for all the trouble she caused you, too!"

Later that afternoon, Dan came jumping out of school.

"You've cheered up!" Mrs. Wilson said.

"I'm feeling lots better!" said Dan. "Come on, Billy! Let's run!"

Billy looked at Mrs. Wilson and said, "Did you know that Dan's the best detective *ever*?"

And he and Dan ran all the way home together.

About the author

Vivian French spent 10 years
working as an actor and writer in
children's theater. She has been a
storyteller in schools for many years
and started writing children's stories
in 1990. Since then, she has had
more than 200 books published.

Look for More *Read-it!* Chapter Books

Alice Goes to Hollywood 1-4048-1678-X
Bricks for Breakfast 1-4048-1275-X
Buffalo Bert: The Cowboy Grandad 1-4048-1660-7
Duncan and the Pirates 1-4048-1277-6
Hetty the Yeti 1-4048-1276-8
The Mean Team from Mars 1-4048-1274-1
Milo in a Mess 1-4048-1679-8
Spookball Champions 1-4048-1278-4
Toby and His Old Tin Tub 1-4048-1279-2
Treasure at the Flea Market 1-4048-1661-5

Looking for a specific title? A complete list
of *Read-it!* Chapter Books is available on our Web site:
www.picturewindowbooks.com